TOEIC

練習測驗（14）

聽力錄音QR碼（1~100題）

U0084647

LISTENING TEST

In the Listening test, you will be asked to demonstrate how well you understand spoken English. The entire Listening test will last approximately 45 minutes. There are four parts, and directions are given for each part. You must mark your answers on the separate answer sheet. Do not write your answers in your test book.

PART 1

Directions: For each question in this part, you will hear four statements about a picture in your test book. When you hear the statements, you must select the one statement that best describes what you see in the picture. Then find the number of the question on your answer sheet and mark your answer. The statements will not be printed in your test book and will be spoken only one time.

Statement (C), "They're sitting at a table," is the best description of the picture, so you should select answer (C) and mark it on your answer sheet.

1.

2.

GO ON TO THE NEXT PAGE.

3.

4.

5.

6.

GO ON TO THE NEXT PAGE.

PART 2

Directions: You will hear a question or statement and three responses spoken in English. They will not be printed in your test book and will be spoken only one time. Select the best response to the question or statement and mark the letter (A), (B), or (C) on your answer sheet.

7. Mark your answer on your answer sheet.

8. Mark your answer on your answer sheet.

9. Mark your answer on your answer sheet.

10. Mark your answer on your answer sheet.

11. Mark your answer on your answer sheet.

12. Mark your answer on your answer sheet.

13. Mark your answer on your answer sheet.

14. Mark your answer on your answer sheet.

15. Mark your answer on your answer sheet.

16. Mark your answer on your answer sheet.

17. Mark your answer on your answer sheet.

18. Mark your answer on your answer sheet.

19. Mark your answer on your answer sheet.

20. Mark your answer on your answer sheet.

21. Mark your answer on your answer sheet.

22. Mark your answer on your answer sheet.

23. Mark your answer on your answer sheet.

24. Mark your answer on your answer sheet.

25. Mark your answer on your answer sheet.

26. Mark your answer on your answer sheet.

27. Mark your answer on your answer sheet.

28. Mark your answer on your answer sheet.

29. Mark your answer on your answer sheet.

30. Mark your answer on your answer sheet.

31. Mark your answer on your answer sheet.

Directions: You will hear some conversations between two people. You will be asked to answer three questions about what the speakers say in each conversation. Select the best response to each question and mark the letter (A), (B), (C), or (D) on your answer sheet. The conversation will not be printed in your test book and will be spoken only one time.

32. Who are the speakers?
    (A) Doctor and patient.
    (B) Teacher and student.
    (C) Husband and wife.
    (D) Customer and clerk.

33. What does the woman want to do?
    (A) Give the man a CAT scan.
    (B) Take the man's temperature.
    (C) Run more tests on the man.
    (D) Prescribe some medication.

34. How does the man feel about taking an MRI?
    (A) Excited.
    (B) Horrified.
    (C) Apprehensive.
    (D) Enraged.

35. Who are the speakers?
    (A) Lovers.
    (B) Co-workers.
    (C) Siblings.
    (D) Rivals.

36. What does the man offer?
    (A) To bring back lunch for the woman.
    (B) To take the woman out to dinner.
    (C) To help the woman with her work.
    (D) To leave the woman alone.

37. Why does the woman decline?
    (A) She doesn't like the man.
    (B) She isn't hungry.
    (C) She has too much work to do.
    (D) She already has something for lunch.

38. Where do the speakers most likely work?
    (A) At a magazine publisher.
    (B) At an art gallery.
    (C) At a cafe.
    (D) At a bookstore.

39. What problem is being discussed?
    (A) The artist is unhappy.
    (B) The caterers are late.
    (C) The placement of some artwork.
    (D) The arrangement of some flowers.

40. What will the woman most likely do next?
    (A) Move an exhibit.
    (B) Revise a schedule.
    (C) Contact an artist.
    (D) Write an article.

41. What does "running around like a chicken with its head cut off" imply?
    (A) The woman is extremely busy.
    (B) The man is inhumane and cruel.
    (C) The woman is terribly shy.
    (D) The man is nosy and rude.

42. What are the speakers mainly discussing?
    (A) Their jobs.
    (B) Their spouses.
    (C) Their children.
    (D) Their relationship.

43. What does the woman imply?
    (A) Being a parent is no fun.
    (B) Her kids are lazy and spoiled.
    (C) The man should mind his own business.
    (D) She's not getting enough sleep.

GO ON TO THE NEXT PAGE.

44. What are the speakers discussing?
    (A) Friendly gossip.
    (B) An interesting story.
    (C) Financial theory.
    (D) A natural disaster.

45. Why did the snake explode?
    (A) Authorities shot it from a cannon.
    (B) It swallowed a bomb.
    (C) The alligator was too big.
    (D) Too much gas.

46. What does the man imply?
    (A) He doesn't believe the woman's story.
    (B) He is terrified of snakes.
    (C) The story is not interesting.
    (D) He might buy an alligator.

47. Who are the speakers?
    (A) Lovers.
    (B) Co-workers.
    (C) Siblings.
    (D) Rivals.

48. What is the woman doing?
    (A) Watching a news report.
    (B) Studying for an exam.
    (C) Reading in her leisure time.
    (D) Writing a report.

49. What does the man offer?
    (A) To write the report.
    (B) To explain psychometrics.
    (C) To chastise Mr. Roberts.
    (D) To read the woman's first draft of the report.

50. Who does the woman ask to speak with?
    (A) Pauline.
    (B) Greg.
    (C) Marge.
    (D) Bob.

51. Who is Greg?
    (A) Pauline's assistant.
    (B) Alice's assistant.
    (C) Marge's assistant.
    (D) Bob's assistant.

52. What does the woman imply?
    (A) She's not in a hurry to solve her problem.
    (B) She's tired of people going on vacation.
    (C) She's afraid of Pauline.
    (D) She's under a lot of pressure.

53. What are the speakers mainly discussing?
    (A) An online payment.
    (B) A store refund.
    (C) A computer upgrade.
    (D) A printing order.

54. What store policy is mentioned?
    (A) Services must be paid for in cash.
    (B) Deliveries must be scheduled in advance.
    (C) Customers must use a shop design.
    (D) Customers must have a shop account.

55. What does the manager explain to the customer?
    (A) An extra charge will be added.
    (B) An account has been suspended.
    (C) A warranty cannot be extended.
    (D) Replacement parts have not arrived.

56. Who are the speakers?
    (A) Teachers.
    (B) Volunteers.
    (C) Lawyers.
    (D) Journalists.

57. How does the man know Terry Bull?
    (A) They were roommates in law school.
    (B) They are from the same town.
    (C) They work for the same company.
    (D) They both dated Paige Turner.

58. What does the woman say about Terry Bull?
    (A) He's in line for a promotion.
    (B) He's a talented judge.
    (C) He's in Peoria.
    (D) He's got an unfortunate name.

59. What problem does the woman have?
    (A) She lost a close relative.
    (B) Her credit card was stolen.
    (C) The credit card was declined in a restaurant.
    (D) Thieves ransacked her apartment.

60. What does the woman want to do?
    (A) Get a credit extension.
    (B) Report a suspicious character.
    (C) Buy a new purse.
    (D) Cancel a stolen credit card.

61. What does the woman imply?
    (A) She misplaced the credit card.
    (B) The credit card was in the stolen purse.
    (C) Her spending limit is too low.
    (D) Everything is always her fault.

___

62. What is the woman's problem?
    (A) She lost her debit card.
    (B) She forgot her PIN number.
    (C) She is lost.
    (D) She can't access her accounts.

63. What does the man ask?
    (A) If the woman has an account with Universal Bank.
    (B) If the woman knows her PIN number.
    (C) If the woman can wait while he transfers the call.
    (D) If the woman has the debit card in her possession.

64. Who does the woman need to speak with?
    (A) A sales representative.
    (B) Someone at United Bank.
    (C) The man's superior.
    (D) A Universal Bank customer service agent.

65. What are the speakers discussing?
    (A) Gift-giving ideas.
    (B) Holiday plans.
    (C) The state of the economy.
    (D) Their kids.

66. What does the woman imply?
    (A) Her family will not have an extravagant holiday celebration this year.
    (B) Her holiday plans are complicated.
    (C) Her kids are spoiled and rude.
    (D) Her husband is a cheapskate who doesn't believe in Santa Claus.

67. What does the man imply?
    (A) He and his wife aren't getting along.
    (B) He is trying to lose weight.
    (C) He doesn't have a lot of money to spend on gifts.
    (D) He never really liked the Christmas season.

___

68. What does Ethan want to do?
    (A) Attend a live broadcast.
    (B) Request a transfer.
    (C) Change a work shift.
    (D) Refer a friend for employment.

69. Why does the woman say, "Oliver has been here a long time."?
    (A) To indicate that Oliver could answer a question.
    (B) To suggest that Oliver be promoted.
    (C) To explain a project Oliver is working on.
    (D) To express surprise about a mistake Oliver made.

70. What does Oliver recommend doing?
    (A) Consulting an organization chart.
    (B) Speaking to a manager.
    (C) Visiting a website.
    (D) Picking up an employee handbook.

___

GO ON TO THE NEXT PAGE.

Directions: You will hear some talks given by a single speaker. You will be asked to answer three questions about what the speaker says in each talk. Select the best response to each question and mark the letter (A), (B), (C), or (D) on your answer sheet. The talks will not be printed in your test book and will be spoken only one time.

71. Who is being introduced?
(A) An actor.
(B) An author.
(C) A politician.
(D) A movie director.

72. What will P.J. Adams most likely talk about?
(A) Her education.
(B) Her new book.
(C) Her religion.
(D) Her children.

73. How many times has P.J. Adams appeared on the program prior to this introduction?
(A) Never.
(B) One.
(C) Two.
(D) A dozen.

74. What is being advertised?
(A) Carpeting.
(B) Furniture.
(C) Home appliances.
(D) Windows.

75. What does Pella guarantee?
(A) Complete customer satisfaction.
(B) Savings of 50 percent on heating bills.
(C) Shatter-proof glass.
(D) Same day installation.

76. How much can the consumer save on installation?
(A) 20 percent.
(B) 25 percent.
(C) 40 percent.
(D) 50 percent.

77. What is the main purpose of the message?
(A) To make a bid.
(B) To file an estimate.
(C) To apologize for a mistake.
(D) To answer questions.

78. What is not included in the estimate?
(A) Carpeting in the conference room.
(B) A range of different types of lighting.
(C) Painting costs.
(D) New windows in the conference room.

79. What does the speaker say Ms. White can do?
(A) Write a check.
(B) Call him back.
(C) Negotiate with the painters.
(D) Give an estimate.

80. Who is the speaker?
(A) A corporate executive.
(B) A sales clerk.
(C) A cashier.
(D) A parking lot attendant.

81. What is the speaker talking about?
(A) Shoplifting.
(B) Advertising.
(C) Health care.
(D) Saving money.

82. Which of the following is NOT part of the speaker's plan?
(A) Cutting labor costs.
(B) Conserving energy.
(C) Reducing profit margins.
(D) Hiring new employees.

83. Who is the speaker most likely talking to?
    (A) Department managers.
    (B) New employees.
    (C) Stockholders.
    (D) Computer instructors.

84. Why are some staff members not taking advantage of the classes?
    (A) They can't afford them.
    (B) They are not convenient.
    (C) They start too early.
    (D) They don't like the instructors.

85. What did the speaker do to solve the problem?
    (A) He arranged for on-site classes.
    (B) He cancelled the classes.
    (C) He gave bonuses.
    (D) He made attendance mandatory.

86. When was this report made?
    (A) At dawn.
    (B) Mid-morning.
    (C) Noon.
    (D) Mid-afternoon.

87. What is causing the back-up in the northbound lanes of Interstate 5?
    (A) People slowing down to look at the accident in the southbound lanes.
    (B) Police and emergency crews.
    (C) Tasty Oatmeal.
    (D) An overturned truck carrying thousands of empty bottles.

88. What will listeners hear next?
    (A) An advertisement.
    (B) The weather report.
    (C) The traffic report.
    (D) A musical performance.

89. What is the speaker announcing?
    (A) A change of working hours.
    (B) A plan to consume more energy.
    (C) A daycare program for employees with young kids.
    (D) A new questionnaire to be passed out.

90. What will happen on Fridays?
    (A) A government official will visit the campus.
    (B) The light bulbs will be changed.
    (C) The office will be closed.
    (D) Employees will go home at 6:00 p.m.

91. How many hours will employees now work per week?
    (A) 10.
    (B) 15.
    (C) 20.
    (D) 40.

92. What is being advertised?
    (A) A product.
    (B) A service.
    (C) A school.
    (D) A job opening.

93. What is suggested about Career Match dot com?
    (A) It is local.
    (B) It is affordable.
    (C) It is old.
    (D) It is effective.

94. What does the speaker suggest listeners do?
    (A) Give their two-week notice.
    (B) Send in their resumes.
    (C) Call or visit the website.
    (D) Show up on time.

GO ON TO THE NEXT PAGE.

```
TOUR SCHEDULE
-------------------------------
Greenbriar District  10:00 A.M.
Lunch  12:00 P.M.
Sears Building  1:15 P.M.
Exploration Museum  4:00 P.M.
============================
```

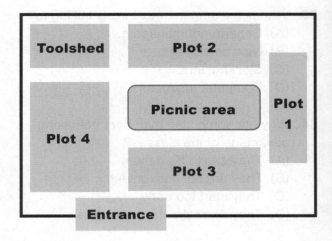

95. What does the speaker say about Shipley's Inn?
(A) It serves exotic food.
(B) It has multiple locations in the area.
(C) It used to be a courthouse.
(D) It has recently won an award.

96. Look at the graphic. What time is this talk most likely being given?
(A) At 10:00 A.M.
(B) At 12:00 P.M.
(C) At 1:15 P.M.
(D) At 4:00 P.M.

97. What does the speaker say she will distribute?
(A) Bottles of water.
(B) Maps.
(C) Brochures.
(D) Umbrellas.

98. Who is the speaker?
(A) A security guard.
(B) A project coordinator.
(C) A course instructor.
(D) A news journalist.

99. Look at the graphic. Where will vegetables be planted?
(A) Plot 1.
(B) Plot 2.
(C) Plot 3.
(D) Plot 4.

100. What does the speaker plan to do on Saturday?
(A) Take some photographs.
(B) Install a fence.
(C) Lead a tour.
(D) Attend a picnic.

This is the end of the Listening test. Turn to Part 5 in your test book.

READING TEST

In the Reading test, you will read a variety of texts and answer several different types of reading comprehension questions. The entire Reading test will last 75 minutes. There are three parts, and directions are given for each part. You are encouraged to answer as many questions as possible within the time allowed.

You must mark your answers on the separate answer sheet. Do not write your answers in your test book.

PART 5

Directions: A word or phrase is missing in each of the sentences below. Four answer choices are given below each sentence. Select the best answer to complete the sentence. Then mark the letter (A), (B), (C), or (D) on your answer sheet.

101. If you really want something in life, you have to work -------.
(A) from it
(B) of it
(C) for it
(D) off it

102. The box is ------- heavy for my grandmother to carry.
(A) many
(B) much too
(C) a lot
(D) little

103. His inability to learn another language was a(n) ------- to his success.
(A) obstacle
(B) pothole
(C) detour
(D) shortcut

104. Night after night, he came home ------- an empty house.
(A) on
(B) at
(C) in
(D) to

105. Our trip to Thailand was ------- inexpensive.
(A) quietly
(B) surprisingly
(C) radically
(D) gently

106. The powerful storm downed two power lines and ------- several large trees.
(A) uprooted
(B) unfurnished
(C) upbraided
(D) undated

107. Hank's interest in Monica seems to ------- at random.
(A) come and go
(B) came and went
(C) high and dry
(D) back and forth

108. We should willingly take risks in ------- of new projects.
(A) supporting
(B) support
(C) supportive
(D) supportable

GO ON TO THE NEXT PAGE.

109. The defunct NASA satellite is expected to fall back to earth ------- days.
(A) with
(B) without
(C) within
(D) withhold

110. Consider all the possibilities ------- making a decision.
(A) until
(B) instead
(C) prior to
(D) as

111. Management is thinking of ------- our main office to Taipei.
(A) appointing
(B) outplaying
(C) deploying
(D) relocating

112. The risks and side effects of using painkillers ------- nausea, headaches, and fever.
(A) invite
(B) intend
(C) inspire
(D) include

113. ------- it was a holiday, Eric went to the office to finish an important project.
(A) Even though
(B) Instead
(C) So
(D) During

114. The film has been nominated for many -------, including the Academy Award for Best Original Screenplay.
(A) demands
(B) respects
(C) honors
(D) memorials

115. More jobs means ------- people looking for work.
(A) farther
(B) further
(C) fewer
(D) faster

116. You can play computer games ------- your homework is finished.
(A) as far as
(B) as long as
(C) as well as
(D) as good as

117. The national spelling bee was won by a ------- girl from Texas.
(A) fourteen-years-old
(B) fourteen-year-old
(C) fourteen-year
(D) fourteen-old

118. Even if you don't organize your files, if you keep all the records in one place, you can sort them out ------- necessary.
(A) where
(B) when
(C) while
(D) which

119. Beijing has announced that it will open two new parts of the Great Wall of China to meet high tourist -------.
(A) protest
(B) outrage
(C) demand
(D) order

120. Tim ------- fourteen, sometimes sixteen, hours a day.
(A) work
(B) works
(C) have worked
(D) is work

121. Our ------- leaves at eight o'clock, so we better head for the airport around five.
    (A) journey
    (B) sight
    (C) travel
    (D) flight

122. Though racial ------- was common in the past, it is no longer tolerated in our society.
    (A) palpitation
    (B) sterilization
    (C) discrimination
    (D) localization

123. The two main ------- of living downtown are the noise and pollution. Otherwise, it's very convenient.
    (A) pullbacks
    (B) fallbacks
    (C) drawbacks
    (D) outbacks

124. There is no evidence to suggest the Mayans believed the world would ------- in December 2012.
    (A) bend
    (B) friend
    (C) end
    (D) send

125. Do you know how much ------- I would need to mail this package to France?
    (A) postage
    (B) weight
    (C) tape
    (D) flight

126. Practical applications of alchemy produced a ------- of contributions to medicine and the physical sciences.
    (A) wide range
    (B) broad stripe
    (C) vast divide
    (D) long road

127. Many critics have tried to ------- the economic recession on the President's domestic policies.
    (A) blame
    (B) list
    (C) correspond
    (D) fault

128. Scott had all ------- of problems in school.
    (A) sights
    (B) sorts
    (C) sizes
    (D) styles

129. The employees ------- about the CEO's resignation before the announcement was made public.
    (A) know
    (B) knew
    (C) knowing
    (D) have known

130. Far from being a shrinking violet, Lucy has many strong ------- which she is not afraid to express.
    (A) opinions
    (B) decisions
    (C) clues
    (D) theories

GO ON TO THE NEXT PAGE.

PART 6

Directions: Read the texts that follow. A word, phrase, or sentence is missing in parts of each text. Four answer choices are given below each of the texts. Select the best answer to complete the text. Then mark the letter (A), (B), (C), or (D) on your answer sheet.

Questions 131-134 refer to the following notice.

AGX Industries
3-D Printer Policy

This 3-D printer is for the ------- use of Graphic Design Department
131.

employees only. Workers from other departments must use the

standard printers found on the second floor. Graphic Design

Department staff members may print up to 5 objects per week

without a manager's authorization. Staff must receive managerial

approval to make ------- items.
132.

Note that 3-D printing ------- for development and business purposes
133.

only. No personal printing is permitted. -------.
134.

Thank you for your cooperation.

131. (A) peculiar
(B) unusual
(C) customary
(D) exclusive

132. (A) additional
(B) required
(C) such
(D) these

133. (A) is intended
(B) should intend
(C) intends
(D) intending

134. (A) The LED monitors have been upgraded to retina screens
(B) The second-floor vending machine will be replaced during the month of September
(C) Objects created with the 3-D printer are for internal use by Convex Labs and external marketing associates
(D) Technical Support maintains all printers and copiers

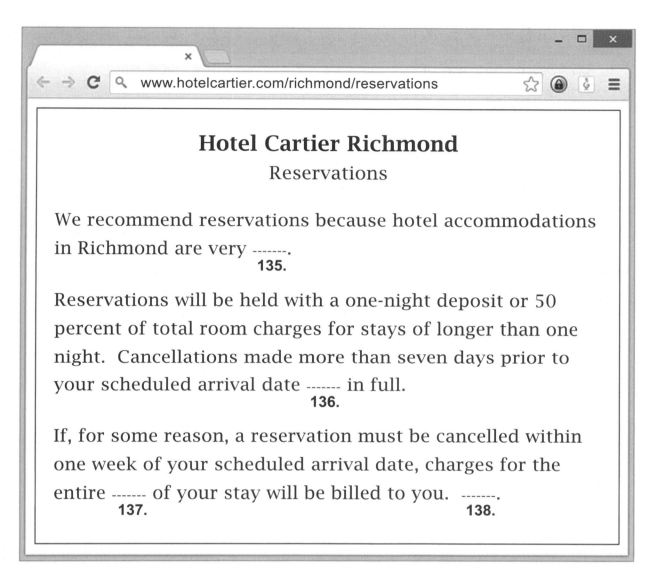

Hotel Cartier Richmond
Reservations

We recommend reservations because hotel accommodations in Richmond are very ------- .
135.

Reservations will be held with a one-night deposit or 50 percent of total room charges for stays of longer than one night. Cancellations made more than seven days prior to your scheduled arrival date ------- in full.
136.

If, for some reason, a reservation must be cancelled within one week of your scheduled arrival date, charges for the entire ------- of your stay will be billed to you. ------- .
137. **138.**

135. (A) limits
(B) limited
(C) limitation
(D) limiting

136. (A) are refunding
(B) had been refunding
(C) will be refunded
(D) were refunded

137. (A) area
(B) height
(C) length
(D) sense

138. (A) This policy applies to early departure as well
(B) In addition, we will soon open another hotel in Richmond
(C) We hope that you have enjoyed your stay
(D) Hotel guests may also purchase these items through room service.

GO ON TO THE NEXT PAGE.

Questions 139-142 refer to the following e-mail.

New Message   _ / x

To   EveryWear Customer Support

Subject: Order EW-098911

To Whom It May Concern:

I recently purchased an all-weather rain jacket from the EveryWear clothing website. When I first received the jacket a month and a half ago, I tried it on and put it in my closet. -------, when I went to wear it in the rain for the first
                                                    139.
time yesterday, I noticed slight defects in the stitching of the hood, causing it to seep moisture. I know that any ------- items must be returned or exchanged
                                                    140.
within three days and that my purchase is no longer within the required time frame. -------. If it ------- out since I checked, I would be happy to choose
        141.   **142.**
another jacket at the same price.

Please let me know what my options are.

Sincerely,
Maggie O'Connor

Sans Serif / B / U / ▤ ▤ ▤ / ‖

Send   🗑 | ▾

139. (A) Still
     (B) However
     (C) Therefore
     (D) Additionally

140. (A) accepted
     (B) ill-fitting
     (C) mistaken
     (D) defective

141. (A) This policy has been extended to at least 60 days
     (B) Nevertheless, I am asking you to kindly make an exception
     (C) Please add a credit to my account to be used for future purchases
     (D) I sent the package back to you two weeks after I received it

142. (A) be selling
     (B) having been sold
     (C) has sold
     (D) will sell

Kimberton to buy Helios Energy manufacturing division

HOUSTON—Kimberton Group LP announced Tuesday that ------- would purchase Helios
143.
Energy Corp. in a deal valued at $230 million.

A spokesperson for Kimberton said the company expects to double its profits by the end of next year. It will accomplish this by making full use of Helios Energy's recently updated manufacturing facilities. -------.
144.

Financial experts believe the Helios Energy acquisition will make Kimberton the world's leading producer of industrial rubber. "They will be well ahead of their -------," said top analyst J.
145.
Walker White.

Kimberton plans to maintain Helios Energy's current workforce, with each of Helios Energy's factories continuing normal operations for the next five years. -------, Kimberton will
146.
evaluate whether additional staff are needed.

143. (A) it
(B) he
(C) those
(D) someone

144. (A) Offers from other firms were rejected
(B) All four are operating at maximum capacity
(C) Another company will be acquired next year
(D) The transaction should improve morale

145. (A) critics
(B) suppliers
(C) competitors
(D) investors

146. (A) As you requested
(B) As a matter of fact
(C) After all
(D) After that time

GO ON TO THE NEXT PAGE.

PART 7

Directions: In this part you will read a selection of texts, such as magazine and newspaper articles, e-mails, and instant messages. Each text or set of texts is followed by several questions. Select the best answer for each question and mark the letter (A), (B), (C), or (D) on your answer sheet.

Questions 147-148 refer to the following invitation.

Shh, it's a surprise...

Dennis Flynn

is turning 50 and he doesn't want anyone

to know about it.

But we're throwing him a surprise party anyway.

Friday, July 17 at 7:30 p.m.

Ruth's Chris Steakhouse, 23 Broad Street, New Orleans

Dress code: business casual

Please, NO GIFTS!

RSVP before July 16 to Vera Flynn via e-mail only!

Flynn.vera@gmail.com

147. What is the purpose of the invitation?
(A) A wedding.
(B) A concert.
(C) A charity dinner.
(D) A surprise party.

148. What is the dress code?
(A) No gifts.
(B) July 16.
(C) Business casual.
(D) Via e-mail only.

Questions 149-150 refer to the following schedule.

THE SUPERSTAR CINEPLEX

Wilshire and Normandy   Los Angeles

NOW SHOWING!

THE BLOB (PG)
starring Rosie O'Donnell
Weekdays only: 12:00, 3:30, 7:00

CRUISIN' FOR A BRUISIN' (NC-17)
starring Adam Lambert and Clay Aiken
12:30, 3:00, 5:30, 8:00

SAW 73 (R) starring Brooklyn Beckham as "The Saw"
Weekdays: 8:00, 10:00   Sat-Sun 7:30, 9:30, 11:30

DATE NIGHT PROMO DEAL

 Buy two (2) tickets before 6:00 p.m. for any feature
and receive a free small popcorn

149. Which of the following is NOT a show time for "The Blob"?
   (A) Monday 12:00.
   (B) Wednesday 3:30.
   (C) Thursday 7:00.
   (D) Saturday 7:00.

150. Who is eligible for a free small popcorn?
   (A) Anyone who buys two tickets.
   (B) Anyone who buys two tickets before 6:00 p.m.
   (C) Anyone who buys a ticket.
   (D) Anyone on a date.

GO ON TO THE NEXT PAGE.

Questions 151-152 refer to the following advertisement.

15cm x 3col

151. What is being advertised?
  (A) A college scholarship.
  (B) A travel package.
  (C) English language courses.
  (D) An art school.

152. How can the admission forms and course details be obtained?
  (A) By going to the main office.
  (B) By request via air mail.
  (C) By downloading them from the Internet.
  (D) By October 10th.

Potter Valley
Park and Camp Ground

Permits are required for:
- Urban camping
- Alcohol consumption
- Open flames (including BBQ grills)

The following are PROHIBITED:
- Motor vehicles (except in parking lot)
- Firearms (no exceptions)
- Amplified sounds
- Alcohol consumption (except by permit)
- Glass containers
- Golfing, swimming, diving
- Drug possession or trafficking

Pets:
- Leash required
- Please clean up after

Enjoy our parks!
Please recycle and dispose of trash properly.
These rules and regulations are enforceable by law.
Mariposa County Department of Parks and Recreation

153. Which of the following does NOT require a permit?
(A) Urban camping.
(B) Alcohol consumption.
(C) Open flames.
(D) Pets.

154. Which of the following is NOT prohibited?
(A) BBQ grills.
(B) Firearms.
(C) Glass containers.
(D) Amplified sound.

GO ON TO THE NEXT PAGE.

Dear Sally,

I have been married 9 years. My husband and I are educated and successful in our careers. We have a daughter, now 15, from my previous marriage as well as two children of our own. My husband loves my daughter and treats her like his own child. My in-laws, however, have never accepted my daughter as a grandchild.

They enjoy our two younger children and play grandparents to them every chance they can. They want to have the little ones sleep over soon and they always call to ask about them. They never mention my daughter. They never send my daughter cards or gifts but do send them to the two little ones.

My husband has told them how their rejection of her hurts me. They have been defensive about it, and have not changed. Now, we are moving closer to them this summer. When we called to discuss this with them, my mother-in-law started crying on the phone saying that she hasn't done anything wrong. I don't want them in our lives if they can't treat all the children the same. Help!

—*Stuck in the Middle*

155. What is the sender's main problem?
(A) Her husband is having an affair.
(B) Her in-laws are very nosy.
(C) Her in-laws don't accept her daughter.
(D) Her in-laws are spoiling her kids.

156. What happened when she tried to discuss the problem with family members?
(A) Her mother-in-law started crying.
(B) Her father-in-law promised a fresh start.
(C) Her daughter threw a temper tantrum.
(D) Her husband told her to shut up.

157. Why is this problem becoming more urgent?
(A) Stuck in the Middle is having another child.
(B) Stuck in the Middle's husband filed for divorce.
(C) Stuck in the Middle's family is moving closer to the in-laws.
(D) Stuck in the Middle's daughter can't sleep at night.

An American hitchhiker who claimed to have been a victim of a drive-by shooting while gathering material for a memoir on kindness actually shot himself, likely to draw publicity to his project, police said. Ray Dolin originally reported to police that he was hitchhiking along a rural Montana road when the driver of a pickup truck pulled up next to him and shot him for no apparent reason. A man driving a pickup truck that matched Dolin's description of the alleged shooter's vehicle was subsequently arrested. Dolin later admitted to police that he had shot himself, and the charges against the man arrested for the shooting have been dropped.

158. What was Ray Dolin doing when he claimed to have been shot?
(A) Writing.
(B) Driving a pick-up truck.
(C) Filing a police report.
(D) Hitchhiking.

159. What do we know about Ray Dolin?
(A) He is well-traveled.
(B) He is very kind.
(C) He shot himself.
(D) He enjoys hitchhiking.

160. What happened to the man Ray Dolin falsely accused?
(A) He died of wounds suffered in the gunfight.
(B) He was arrested and later released.
(C) He left the state of Montana and is now considered a fugitive.
(D) He wrote a memoir about kindness.

GO ON TO THE NEXT PAGE.

Contract for Purchase of a Car

Buyer's Name   Seller's Name

Address   Address

City, State, ZIP   City, State, ZIP

Phone   Phone

The Seller hereby conveys to the Buyer full ownership and title to the motor vehicle described below:

Description of Motor Vehicle Sold:

Year _____ Make _____ Model _____

VIN: _____

The Buyer hereby agrees to pay the Seller $_____ on (/ /20), and $_____ on the _____th day of each month beginning (/ /20), until all payments made to the Seller total $_____.

If Buyer fails to make a payment on or before its due date, a late fee of $_____ shall be added to the balance due and shall be payable immediately.

Both parties hereby agree that this is an "as-is" sale, with no warranties of any kind expressed or implied.

This agreement shall be governed by the laws of the State of _____ and the County of _____ and any applicable U.S. laws.

The parties hereby signify their agreement to the terms above by their signatures affixed below:

_____   _____

Buyer's signature, date   Seller's signature, date

161. What is the purpose of this contract?
(A) Property rental.
(B) Security clearance.
(C) Construction estimate.
(D) Purchase of a car.

162. Who is the contract between?
(A) The county and the state.
(B) The Department of Motor Vehicles.
(C) Buyer and Seller.
(D) Year, make, and model.

163. What do both parties agree to?
(A) This is an "as-is" sale with no warranties.
(B) To complete all payments within one year.
(C) Shared ownership of the vehicle.
(D) Laws of the county come before those of the state.

Crime dramas are fun, engaging and entertaining to watch, but is it possible that they cause more harm than good? The tremendous popularity of television shows like "Crime Scene Investigators: Miami" (CSI) have gone a long way toward building interest in the field of forensic science and crime scene investigations, but there may be a downside. There is a concern among the forensic science and law enforcement communities that the technology and tactics presented in these shows have led to unrealistic expectations about police capabilities among the public at large and, even worse, potential jurors.

The "CSI effect" is a term applied to the increasingly pervasive idea that criminal cases can be wrapped up in an hour and that there is always incontrovertible proof of guilt available. While it's true that great advances have been made in the area of forensic science, it's unrealistic to expect a crime scene to be processed, evidence analyzed and a conclusive forensics report to be completed before the detective or criminal investigator assigned to the case gets back to the office after leaving the scene.

Unfortunately, though, that is what many victims expect, and what a lot of juries now look for. When they don't see it, defense attorneys often exploit the lack of DNA or other smoking gun evidence in an effort to make it appear as though law enforcement investigators didn't do their job. Usually, though, nothing could be further from the truth.

164. What is the main result of the "CSI effect"?
(A) People living in poor areas are afraid of the police.
(B) Modern technology makes solving crimes a slam dunk.
(C) People have developed unrealistic expectations about solving crimes.
(D) Police work seems glamorous and entertaining.

165. What has caused the "CSI effect"?
(A) Urban legend.
(B) Television programming.
(C) Popular opinion.
(D) Scientific research.

166. Where would this article most likely be found?
(A) In a sports magazine.
(B) In a cable television guide.
(C) In a journal of psychology.
(D) In a book of exotic recipes.

167. According to the author, who uses the "CSI effect" to their advantage?
(A) Criminals.
(B) Crime scene investigators.
(C) Forensic scientists.
(D) Defense attorneys.

GO ON TO THE NEXT PAGE.

Questions 168-171 refer to the following report.

In a bad mood? Don't worry—according to research, it's good for you. An American psychology expert who has been studying emotions has found being grumpy makes us think more clearly. In contrast to those annoying happy types, miserable people are better at decision-making and less gullible, his experiments showed. While cheerfulness promotes creativity, gloominess breeds attentiveness and careful thinking, Professor Michael Callahan told Colorado Science Magazine. The University of Denver researcher says a grumpy person can cope with more demanding situations than a happy one because of the way the brain "promotes information processing strategies". Professor Callahan asked volunteers to watch different films and dwell on positive or negative events in their life, designed to put them in either a good or bad mood. Next he asked them to take part in a series of tasks, including judging the truth of urban myths and providing eyewitness accounts of events. Those in a bad mood outperformed those who were jolly—they made fewer mistakes and were better communicators. Professor Callahan said: "Whereas a positive mood seems to promote creativity, flexibility, cooperation and reliance on mental shortcuts, negative moods trigger more attentive, careful thinking and paying greater attention to the external world."

168. What is this report mainly about?
(A) Psychology.
(B) Decision making.
(C) Mythology.
(D) Multi-tasking.

169. What does Professor Callahan say about grumpy people?
(A) Their ability to relax is compromised.
(B) Their moods are influenced by others.
(C) They are better communicators than happy people.
(D) They are more creative than happy people.

170. Which of the following is NOT promoted by a positive mood?
(A) Creativity.
(B) Careful thinking.
(C) Cooperation.
(D) Flexibility.

171. Which of the following is promoted by a negative mood?
(A) Attention to detail.
(B) Creating eyewitness accounts.
(C) Gullibility.
(D) Cheerfulness.

Marita Leroy (10:37 A.M.)

I was just asked by the financial officer to sit in on the firm's annual budget review. Therefore, I can't make our 3:00 P.M. meeting today.

Kevin Ambari (10:38 A.M.)

Could we practice tomorrow's client presentation earlier? What about reserving the conference room at 1:00 P.M.?

Dan Collins (10:39 A.M.)

That would be better for me anyway. I need to leave at 4:00 PM for a doctor's appointment.

Marita Leroy (10:39 A.M.)

No such luck. I'm looking at the schedule now—it's booked solid all afternoon.

Kevin Ambari (10:40 A.M.)

Then why don't you both come to my office at 2:00? We can run through the presentation and slideshow here.

Dan Collns (10:41 A.M.)

Sounds good. Should I get a projector from the A/V dept.?

Kevin Ambari (10:42 A.M.)

Don't bother. We can look at the slides on my computer screen.

Marita Leroy (10:43 A.M.)

OK. See you later.

GO ON TO THE NEXT PAGE.

172. Why is Ms. Leroy unavailable at 3:00 P.M.?

(A) She has a phone call with important clients.

(B) She has to give a presentation.

(C) She has been asked to attend a meeting.

(D) She has a medical appointment.

173. At 10:42 A.M., what does Mr. Ambari most likely mean when he writes, "Don't bother."?

(A) He should not be disturbed this afternoon.

(B) Ms. Leroy should not reserve a room.

(C) Mr. Collins does not have to come to a meeting.

(D) Mr. Collins does not need to bring a projector.

174. Why does Mr. Ambari suggest using his office?

(A) Because it can accommodate a lot of people.

(B) Because it is located near the finance office.

(C) Because his audiovisual equipment has been upgraded.

(D) Because the conference room is unavailable.

175. When will the three people meet?

(A) At 1:00 P.M.

(B) At 2:00 P.M.

(C) At 3:00 P.M.

(D) At 4:00 P.M.

Letter 1

Dear Dr. Stein,

I am applying for the Congressional Scholarship, a $10,000 annuity to be awarded to a single student. Given that my enrollment at Harvard is dependent on my receiving financial aid, this would be a wonderful opportunity for me.

The recipient of the scholarship must demonstrate both ability and direction in his or her field of study. In order to assess such qualities, the scholarship committee requires that applicants submit at least one reference letter from a professor in their major department. Would you do me the honor of submitting the reference letter required for the application?

I took your International Law class in the fall semester of 2017, and your Global Organization class in the spring of 2018. I received an A in both classes.

All scholarship materials must be submitted by November 30, and I enclosed an addressed, stamped envelope for your convenience. The addressee on the letter should be Scholarship Director Ogden Chalmers. I will be stopping by during your office hours this week to confirm. Meanwhile, if you need to speak with me directly, I can be reached at (650) 323-9826.

Appreciatively,
Louis Langer

GO ON TO THE NEXT PAGE.

Letter 2

Dear Director Chalmers,

One of my best and brightest students, Louis Langer, is applying for the Congressional Scholarship. It is my opinion that Mr. Langer is an excellent candidate for the award in question; he has proven himself to be well-qualified in every facet of the scholarship requirements, both in my classes and elsewhere on campus.

Having served as a professor at Harvard for over two decades, I have had the opportunity to observe some exceptional students. Louis Langer is one of those rare students who manages to stand head and shoulders above the rest, in a highly competitive environment. In my classes with Mr. Langer, namely International Law and Global Organization, he has exhibited deep insight into the world of finance and law. He has an excellent attitude and work ethic, which will no doubt form the foundation of his education.

I might add that I am aware of other professors' opinions regarding Mr. Langer, and to my knowledge, they are in accordance with mine. That is, Louis Langer is the superior choice to be the recipient of the Congressional Scholarship.

Sincerely,
Dr. Stu Stein, Professor Emeritus Law
Harvard University

176. Who is Louis Langer?
    (A) A lawyer.
    (B) A student.
    (C) A doctor.
    (D) A banker.

177. What did Louis Langer ask Dr. Stein to do?
    (A) Change his grade.
    (B) Supply a reference.
    (C) Demonstrate a product.
    (D) Cancel his subscription.

178. How do Louis Langer and Dr. Stein know each other?
    (A) They work at the same firm.
    (B) They are college roommates.
    (C) Louis attended Dr. Stein's classes.
    (D) Dr. Stein married Louis' sister.

179. What did Dr. Stein do in response to the request?
    (A) He wrote the reference.
    (B) He rejected the idea.
    (C) He gave the task to a colleague.
    (D) He looked up Louis Langer on Facebook.

180. What is Dr. Stein's opinion of Louis Langer?
    (A) Louis is a lazy student.
    (B) Louis is a sensitive individual.
    (C) Louis is an exceptional student.
    (D) Louis is too wealthy to receive financial aid.

GO ON TO THE NEXT PAGE.

MEMO

To: Department Heads

From: Deborah Lynn

Date: December 8, 2018

Subject: Annual Bonus Leave for Employees with Outstanding Performance

Starting January 1, we will introduce the following modification in our company policy regarding annual leave (paid vacation). Every year, one employee from each department will be awarded a special bonus leave for outstanding performance.

The eligible employees will have five (5) days of annual leave credited on January 15. The bonus leave will be accounted for separately and will remain available until used, notwithstanding any other limitation of annual leave that may be carried forward.

We will have a meeting on December 15 at 10:00 a.m. to discuss the results of the 2018 performance evaluation and approve the final list of eligible employees.

The announcement will be made to the employees following the meeting. If you have any questions or concerns, please contact me prior to the meeting.

To: "Deborah" < el_queso_grande@cxt.com >
From: "Pete Sears" < oh_no@cxt.com >
Subject: Annual Leave Memo
Date: 12/12/18

Deborah,

I had the chance to sit down with Ron Booker and a couple of the other department heads to discuss the bonus leave policy, and I was chosen as scapegoat to raise a few concerns with you. I don't agree with everyone on some of these sticking points, so please keep in mind the old adage, "Don't shoot the messenger."

1. More than one department head believes the new policy is a bad idea, at least they perceive it to be a bad idea within their individual departments. Their concerns are based on the respective competitive dynamics within their departments. In other words, they are worried that this special bonus might exacerbate an already highly contentious and competitive atmosphere, thereby disturbing the uneasy equilibrium they have managed to hold so far.

2. One department head in particular has bemoaned the awarding of an extra week (five working days) leave when our current leave policy is already generous, perhaps too generous in this individual's opinion. So again, in plain terms, this individual feels that our departments are already strained by absenteeism and regular vacations, and that one more person out for one more week just makes things worse. I would like to note that on this point, I strongly disagree and plan on saying so at the meeting, should this concern be raised.

3. Perhaps the wording of the policy will be cleared up in the meeting but all of us agree that we are confused by the sentence: "The bonus leave will be accounted for separately and will remain available until used, notwithstanding any other limitation of annual leave that may be carried forward." Exactly what does that mean? The leave can be carried over or it cannot be carried over?

Thanks for your time and I look forward to discussing these issues with you.

Yours,
Pete

GO ON TO THE NEXT PAGE.

181. Why did Deborah Lynn send the memo?
- (A) To inform her employees of an impending move.
- (B) To announce a policy change.
- (C) To ask for volunteers.
- (D) To explain a new rule.

182. What will happen at the December 15 meeting?
- (A) They will discuss the annual budget.
- (B) They will review current sick leave policies.
- (C) They will select the employees eligible for the bonus.
- (D) They will decide how much the bonus will be.

183. Why did Pete Sears send the e-mail?
- (A) He was angry about the announcement.
- (B) He was wondering why he didn't get the memo.
- (C) He was happy to hear about the policy change.
- (D) He was chosen by his co-workers to raise their concerns with Deborah.

184. What does Pete Sears strongly disagree with?
- (A) The idea that the employees already have enough vacation time.
- (B) The concept of awarding bonuses for outstanding performance.
- (C) The method by which employees are evaluated.
- (D) The manner in which Deborah announced the change.

185. Which of the following is NOT a concern mentioned in Pete's e-mail?
- (A) The bonus may upset the employee dynamic.
- (B) The employees already get enough leave.
- (C) The wording of the policy change is unclear.
- (D) The performance evaluations may be flawed.

From:	Franklin Steves (PPT U.S.)
To:	Carmen Garcia (PPT Ecuador)
Re:	Delmonico Steel
Date:	May 10

Hello Franklin,

I understand that you are making arrangements for Delmonico Steel's visit from Ecuador in June. I wanted to let you know that we at the PPT Ecuador office have been providing ongoing services for Delmonico Steel's operations here in Quito for the past seven years. Now that they are establishing an office in Miami, they are eager to partner with PPT there as well. Reaching an agreement with them should be fairly straightforward.

Regarding the welcome reception you are planning for June, I am aware that several on Delmonico's negotiating team have very specific food preferences and needs. Please take this into consideration.

Let me know if I can help in any way.

Regards,
Carmen

GO ON TO THE NEXT PAGE.

Choose the very best for your guests for your next celebration.

Top Hat Catering has been providing excellence in service and dining for both casual and formal events in Tampa for over 25 years.

Here is what sets Top Hat Catering apart from its competitors:

- We can adapt all menu items to different dietary restrictions.
- We can arrange live entertainment for your event.
- We provide complete cleanup service after each event.
- We cater events from 12:00 noon to 11:00 P.M., seven days a week, 365 days a year.

Call our reservations hotline at 305-749-1170 to book your event now!

BISCAYNE HOTEL
A WAVERLY INTERNATIONAL PROPERTY

June 8

Dear Mr. Caruso,

Welcome to Tampa. I trust your journey was a pleasant one. Our team would like to invite you and your team to a welcome reception at 7:00 tonight here in the Biscayne Hotel. It will be held in the Causeway Room on the hotel's third floor. Please join us for this dinner so we can get to know each other better in advance of our upcoming business meetings.

If you require any assistance, please contact me at 305-525-3250.

Sincerely,
Franklin Chou

---

186. What is the main purpose of the e-mail?
(A) To revise a client's itinerary.
(B) To review a contract.
(C) To coordinate with another office about a client.
(D) To update a meeting agenda.

187. What makes Top Hat Catering an appropriate vendor for the PPT event?
(A) Its flexible menu.
(B) Its affordability.
(C) Its entertainment options.
(D) Its selection of venues.

189. For what company does Mr. Caruso most likely work?
(A) PPT Ecuador.
(B) Delmonico Steel.
(C) Top Hat Catering.
(D) Waverly International.

188. Based on the information in the advertisement, what kind of event would Top Hat Catering be unlikely to cater?
(A) A holiday dinner.
(B) A birthday party.
(C) A business breakfast.
(D) A wedding reception.

190. When did Mr. Caruso most likely receive the note?
(A) When he checked into his hotel.
(B) When he finished a series of business meetings.
(C) When he arrived at PPT U.S.'s offices.
(D) When he landed at an airport.

GO ON TO THE NEXT PAGE.

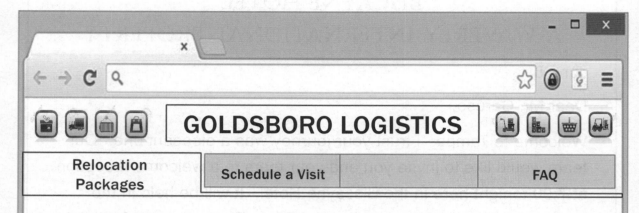

GOLDSBORO LOGISTICS

| Relocation Packages | Schedule a Visit | FAQ |

Choose the relocation package that best suits your needs, then click the "Schedule a Visit" tab to arrange an in-house estimate. Each relocation package comes with an optional storage-space lease plan (SSLP). The SSLP fees listed are valid until 30 June.

Standard: Includes moving truck and crew for up to four hours, ropes and straps, and two handcarts. SSLP fee: $50 first month; $65 every month thereafter.

Superior: Includes all features of the standard package plus boxes and covers for artwork, dishes, TVs, computer accessories, and mattresses. SSLP fee: $60 first month; $75 every month thereafter.

Deluxe: Includes all features of the superior package plus packing and labeling of boxes (content and room location). SSLP fee: $70 first month; $85 every month thereafter.

Premium: Includes all features of the deluxe package plus vacuuming of rooms and removal of carpet stains. SSLP fee: $80 first month; $95 every month thereafter.

From:	Dave Goldsboro
To:	Karen Meeks
Re:	Your Move: First Stage Complete
Date:	May 1

Dear Ms. Meeks,

This is to let you know that your belongings have now been transported from 359 Plainfield Rd. in Woodridge to our storage facility in Downers Grove and placed in a storage unit. Per the terms of your SSLP, they will remain here until May 31, at which time they will be transferred to your new home at 109 Fairfield Rd., Downers Grove.

If you wish to extend your SSLP beyond the current end date of May 31, you must notify us of your decision at least three (3) days in advance. Moreover, for every month that your belongings are stored on our premises beyond May 31, a fee as specified in your SSLP will be automatically charged to your account on the first day of every month.

If you have any questions, please do not hesitate to contact us.

Best regards,
Dave Goldsboro
Goldsboro Logistics

GO ON TO THE NEXT PAGE.

From:	Karen Meeks
To:	Dave Goldsboro
Re:	Your Move: First Stage Complete
Date:	May 2

Dear Mr. Goldsboro,

Thank you for your e-mail. I was very impressed with the courtesy, professionalism, and thoroughness of your crew. Each room, the basement included, was perfectly clean. Even an ink stain that was on the carpet in my home office is now hardly visible.

Please note that due to unforeseen circumstances, our move-in date has changed. We now need our items to be transferred to 109 Fairfield Road on Friday, June 7.

Finally, we would like to confirm that your storage units are climate-controlled. We are worried that an antique table of ours might be ruined if exposed to excessive heat or humidity.

Sincerely,
Karen Meeks

191. According to the webpage, what is true about Goldsboro's storage-space lease plans?
(A) They must be paid for before a home visit is arranged.
(B) They are available for a limited time.
(C) Their rates vary by relocation package.
(D) Their rates change every three months.

192. According to the second e-mail, what is Ms. Meeks concerned about?
(A) A spot on her carpet.
(B) The size of her storage unit.
(C) Damage to her furniture.
(D) The loss of her copy of the SSLP contract.

193. What is the purpose of the first e-mail?
(A) To report on the status of a service.
(B) To request payment.
(C) To answer a customer's question.
(D) To communicate an invoicing error.

194. What service package did Ms. Meeks most likely choose?
(A) Standard.
(B) Superior.
(C) Deluxe.
(D) Premium.

195. What is implied about Goldsboro Logistics?
(A) It cannot meet Ms. Meeks's request.
(B) It will charge Ms. Meeks an additional fee on June 1.
(C) Its Woodridge facility will be relocating to Downers Grove.
(D) Its crew has often been praised for its professionalism.

GO ON TO THE NEXT PAGE.

LA Phil
CENTENNIAL CAMPAIGN 100

Support LA PHIL

The Los Angeles Philharmonic is entering its 100th year of presenting world-class musical performances. Please help us continue this tradition by becoming a Philharmonic sponsor. Your financial support will enable us to maintain low ticket prices and keep our music accessible to everyone.

You receive many special benefits in exchange for your financial donation. The list below shows the benefits offered at each level of support.

Patron Sponsor ($100 - $399):
Receive the music CD *The Delightful Sounds of the Los Angeles Philharmonic* and a one-year subscription to *California Music Spotlight* (published six times annually).

Season Sponsor ($400 - $999):
Receive *The Delightful Sounds of the Los Angeles Philharmonic*, a one-year subscription to *California Music Spotlight* and a 15% discount on all LA PHIL concert tickets.

Masterworks Sponsor ($1000 or more):
Receive Season Sponsor benefits, special reserved seating, and the opportunity to dine with the Philharmonic conductor James Colby-Ross at LA PHIL's annual musicians' dinner.

Please send your donation to: Support LA PHIL, 801 S. 7th Street, Los Angeles, CA 90021. To learn about more ways to support the Los Angeles Philharmonic, please call our support coordinator Jennifer Carmichael at 323-545-2813, or write to her at the address above.

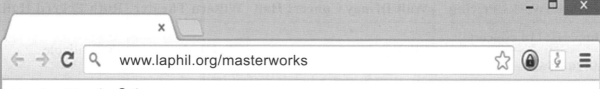

Southern California Times Masterworks

It's the 100th anniversary of The Los Angeles Philharmonic. We can't celebrate without you!

Music Director Michael Cavaleri is pulling out all the stops for our premier Southern California Times Masterworks series, with some of the most demanding masterpieces in history to showcase your virtuoso Los Angeles Philharmonic. With concerts in L.A., San Diego, and Santa Barbara, the Southern California Times Masterworks series is available in packages of 14, 10, 7 and 5 concerts, including our new matinee series at the Wiltern Theater. As a subscriber, you receive premium seating at the same low ticket prices for the top tier $30 and $45 seats at each concert.

Subscribers continue to enjoy free flexible ticket exchanges, free friend vouchers, a 10% discount on additional ticket purchases, and advance notice for best seats to our concert specials. Pro-rated packages are now available. To order your subscription, click the series links below to purchase online or call the LA PHIL Ticket Center at 727.892.3337 or 1.800.662.7286 Monday through Friday, 9:00 AM to 5:00 PM, or Saturday and Sunday, 10:00 AM to 3:00 PM. You can also contact the Ticket Center by e-mail at **ticketcenter@laphil.org**.

For a PDF version of the Masterworks series, **click here**. For a PDF version of the series break out, **click here**.

GO ON TO THE NEXT PAGE.

Masterworks Pricing	Walt Disney Concert Hall	Wiltern Theater	Ruth Eckerd Hall
Imperial (14 concerts) $420 - $630	**Click to buy**	**Click to buy**	not available
Intermezzo (10 concerts) $450 - $300	**Click to buy**	**Click to buy**	**Click to buy**
Fanfare (7 concerts) $315 - $210	not available	not available	not available
Ovation (7 concerts) $315 - $210	**Click to buy**	**Click to buy**	**Click to buy**
Matinees (5 concerts) $225 - $150	**Click to buy**	**Click to buy**	not available

196. What is the main purpose of the advertisement?
(A) To solicit donations.
(B) To announce a new schedule.
(C) To introduce a new musician.
(D) To promote an upcoming festival.

197. What is indicated about The Los Angeles Philharmonic?
(A) It is moving to a new location.
(B) It is celebrating a milestone.
(C) It is funded by local taxes.
(D) It is a for-profit corporation.

198. According to the website, what is new at the Wiltern Theater?
(A) A matinee series.
(B) Premium seating.
(C) Friend vouchers.
(D) Ticket exchanges.

199. What is Michael Cavaleri's role with the LA Phil?
(A) Conductor.
(B) Support coordinator.
(C) Music director.
(D) Magazine publisher.

200. Which Masterworks series is completely sold out?
(A) Imperial.
(B) Intermezzo.
(C) Fanfare.
(D) Ovation.

Stop! This is the end of the test. If you finish before time is called, you may go back to Parts 5, 6, and 7 and check your work.

NO TEST MATERIAL ON THIS PAGE

GO ON TO THE NEXT PAGE.

New TOEIC Listening Script

PART 1

1. (   ) (A) The market is closed.
       (B) The market is crowded.
       (C) The market is dirty.
       (D) The market is empty.

2. (   ) (A) The man is at the beach.
       (B) The woman is at home.
       (C) The man is on a bicycle.
       (D) The woman is on the sidewalk.

3. (   ) (A) The café is full.
       (B) The café is empty.
       (C) The library is busy.
       (D) The school is closed.

4. (   ) (A) The men are fighting.
       (B) The women are seated.
       (C) They are eating dinner.
       (D) This is a private event.

5. (   ) (A) This is a new building.
       (B) This is the site of a funeral.
       (C) This is an ancient landmark.
       (D) This is a museum.

6. (   ) (A) They are factory workers.
       (B) They are a dance group.
       (C) The restaurant is empty.
       (D) They are students in a classroom.

PART 2

7. (   ) Did you hear that?
    (A) I didn't hear anything.
    (B) I've been here for an hour.
    (C) That is neither here nor there.

8. (   ) What's keeping Elaine?
    (A) Dump her.
    (B) She's on the phone with a client.
    (C) I doubt you can keep it up.

9. (   ) Does your teacher speak Chinese in class?
    (A) Not only.
    (B) Never.
    (C) Few.

10. (   ) Did anyone remember to call Mr. Edwards?
    (A) Mr. Edwards is on the phone.
    (B) I left a message this morning.
    (C) Only if I remember.

11. (   ) Can I borrow ten dollars?
    (A) Sorry, I don't have any cash on me.
    (B) It costs ten dollars.
    (C) I'm willing to pay five hundred dollars.

12. (   ) I'm never going to finish the project on time.
    (A) Is there anything I can do to help?
    (B) Did you make it to the finish line?
    (C) You're a quitter.

13. (   ) Are they leaving so soon?
    (A) I'll be right back.
    (B) Yes, I'm afraid so.
    (C) I'm wearing pants.

14. (   ) How many copies of the form do you need?
    (A) Only one.
    (B) Make copies of the form.
    (C) The copier is out of order.

GO ON TO THE NEXT PAGE.

15. (　　) Why are you carrying an umbrella?
　　　　(A) It's supposed to rain this afternoon.
　　　　(B) I've been carrying you for months.
　　　　(C) Don't open it in the house.

16. (　　) Does Marlene always bring doughnuts on Fridays?
　　　　(A) That's why you're getting chubby.
　　　　(B) Like clockwork.
　　　　(C) No, I'm on a diet.

17. (　　) Didn't you use to work at McDonald's?
　　　　(A) Would you like fries with that?
　　　　(B) The Big Mac is very tasty.
　　　　(C) No, I worked at Burger King.

18. (　　) Is that your cousin?
　　　　(A) The play's the thing.
　　　　(B) No, but the resemblance is striking.
　　　　(C) Yes, she is my sister.

19. (　　) Where did you get your haircut?
　　　　(A) I've never been to Harrisburg.
　　　　(B) I started losing it.
　　　　(C) At a barbershop in the mall.

20. (　　) Do you know if Nelson is in town?
　　　　(A) The town is famous for its barbeque.
　　　　(B) He said he would.
　　　　(C) I think he arrives this afternoon.

21. (　　) Has the new software program been installed?
　　　　(A) Get with the program.
　　　　(B) I don't know. Ask somebody in IT.
　　　　(C) Read the manual.

22. (　　) Do you know if we have to work overtime?
　　　　(A) I think we do.
　　　　(B) We get paid overtime.
　　　　(C) I went to work.

23. (　　) Do you like living in New York?
    (A) I've moved many times.
    (B) No, I live in New York.
    (C) Sometimes.

24. (　　) What's your favorite kind of cuisine?
    (A) Desert.
    (B) A sports car.
    (C) Italian.

25. (　　) Have you started sending out your resume?
    (A) Work hard, play hard.
    (B) Yes, I was able to fake it.
    (C) I've sent it to a couple of firms.

26. (　　) Where is your office located?
    (A) Yes, I've been working a lot.
    (B) One-eleven Main Street.
    (C) Come to my office.

27. (　　) How long have you known Daniel?
    (A) He's too short.
    (B) We've known each other since high school.
    (C) His name is Daniel.

28. (　　) Tom, this is my friend, Gary.
    (A) I don't know.
    (B) Look at it.
    (C) We've met.

29. (　　) It's Fred's birthday tomorrow.
    (A) Thanks for reminding me. I need to buy him a gift.
    (B) Not this year.
    (C) We never did see eye to eye.

30. (　　) How much did you pay for the tickets?
    (A) About a week.
    (B) I've been waiting since four.
    (C) Fifteen dollars a piece.

GO ON TO THE NEXT PAGE.

31. (   ) Is this your coat?
          (A) I'll have some.
          (B) Go get it.
          (C) No, that's Nancy's coat.

PART 3

Questions 32 through 34 _refer to the following conversation._

W : The CAT scan appears normal but the blood test was inconclusive. So I'd like to run a few more tests on you, just to be safe.

M : That's fine but… what kind of tests are you talking about?

W : The first test is called an MRI. You lie inside a giant tube, sort of like a tanning bed, and we use lasers to examine your entire body. It will take about an hour.

M : That doesn't sound like fun. I'm kind of claustrophobic. Are you really sure I need it?

32. (   ) Who are the speakers?
          (A) Doctor and patient.
          (B) Teacher and student.
          (C) Husband and wife.
          (D) Customer and clerk.

33. (   ) What does the woman want to do?
          (A) Give the man a CAT scan.
          (B) Take the man's temperature.
          (C) Run more tests on the man.
          (D) Prescribe some medication.

34. (   ) How does the man feel about taking an MRI?
          (A) Excited.
          (B) Horrified.
          (C) Apprehensive.
          (D) Enraged.

Questions 35 through 37 _refer to the following conversation._

M : Hi, Kim. Listen, a new restaurant just opened across the street. I was thinking about trying it. Would you like to have lunch with me?

W : Thanks for the offer, Howard. I'd love to have lunch with you but I'm swamped here.

M : Oh, you're handling the Swanson account, aren't you? Well, how about if I grab something for you while I'm out?

W : Thanks, that's sweet, but I brought my lunch from home today.

35. (   ) Who are the speakers?
     (A) Lovers.
     (B) Co-workers.
     (C) Siblings.
     (D) Rivals.

36. (   ) What does the man offer?
     (A) To bring back lunch for the woman.
     (B) To take the woman out to dinner.
     (C) To help the woman with her work.
     (D) To leave the woman alone.

37. (   ) Why does the woman decline?
     (A) She doesn't like the man.
     (B) She isn't hungry.
     (C) She has too much work to do.
     (D) She already has something for lunch.

Questions 38 through 40 *refer to the following conversation between three speakers.*

Man UK : So, guys, we're all set for the Regina Lawry exhibition tomorrow night. However, I just have to say—I'm concerned about the placement of some paintings.

Man US : Which paintings are you talking about?

Man UK : The whole black and white series. I feel like it's dominating that side of the gallery.

W : Hmm. You're right. Perhaps we could break up the series and place them around the gallery. Is this how the artist wanted the paintings to be displayed?

Man US : If I remember correctly, it is. I'd have to check her original e-mail, but I'm almost positive.

W : I see. Well, I'll call her and see if she can come down to the gallery some time this evening to preview the exhibition. We might be able to convince her to change her mind.

38. (   ) Where do the speakers most likely work?
     (A) At a magazine publisher.
     (B) At an art gallery.
     (C) At a café.
     (D) At a bookstore.

GO ON TO THE NEXT PAGE.

39. (   ) What problem is being discussed?
    (A) The artist is unhappy.
    (B) The caterers are late.
    (C) The placement of some artwork.
    (D) The arrangement of some flowers.

40. (   ) What will the woman most likely do next?
    (A) Move an exhibit.
    (B) Revise a schedule.
    (C) Contact an artist.
    (D) Write an article.

Questions 41 through 43 refer to the following conversation.

M : You look tired. What's going on with you?

W : You have no idea. I'm running around like a chicken with its head cut off. My kids are at that age now where every day is a marathon of activities. School, soccer practice, violin lessons, camping trips, baseball games—it never ends!

M : I hear you. Thankfully, mine are grown up and out of the house. I kind of miss it, you know, all the excitement.

W : Sure, you can say that now. But remember what it was like to get three hours of sleep a night?

41. (   ) What does "running around like a chicken with its head cut off" imply?
    (A) The woman is extremely busy.
    (B) The man is inhumane and cruel.
    (C) The woman is terribly shy.
    (D) The man is nosy and rude.

42. (   ) What are the speakers mainly discussing?
    (A) Their jobs.
    (B) Their spouses.
    (C) Their children.
    (D) Their relationship.

43. (   ) What does the woman imply?
    (A) Being a parent is no fun.
    (B) Her kids are lazy and spoiled.
    (C) The man should mind his own business.
    (D) She's not getting enough sleep.

W : Did you see the story about the giant snake that exploded?

M : No, I didn't get a chance to check the news. What happened?

W : Apparently, a giant python in Florida tried to eat a six-foot alligator. And he got most of the alligator into his belly—but it was too big. Then it just split wide open!

M : No way! That's incredible. Do they have pictures of it?

44. (   ) What are the speakers discussing?
    (A) Friendly gossip.
    (B) An interesting story.
    (C) Financial theory.
    (D) A natural disaster.

45. (   ) Why did the snake explode?
    (A) Authorities shot it from a cannon.
    (B) It swallowed a bomb.
    (C) The alligator was too big.
    (D) Too much gas.

46. (   ) What does the man imply?
    (A) He doesn't believe the woman's story.
    (B) He is terrified of snakes.
    (C) The story is not interesting.
    (D) He might buy an alligator.

M : Wow, Lisa! What's with all the books? Are you studying for an exam?

W : Well, I'm studying but not for an exam. Mr. Roberts asked me to write a report about investment strategies, particularly something called psychometrics.

M : Oh, I know all about it. I majored in psychology before switching to finance. Psychometrics is all about using personality tests and evaluations to make financial decisions.

W : Mr. Roberts really should have had you write the report then. I can't make head or tail of this stuff.

M : Tell you what. If you want, I could look over your first draft and give you some feedback.

GO ON TO THE NEXT PAGE.

47. (　　) Who are the speakers?
    (A) Lovers.
    (B) Co-workers.
    (C) Siblings.
    (D) Rivals.

48. (　　) What is the woman doing?
    (A) Watching a news report.
    (B) Studying for an exam.
    (C) Reading in her leisure time.
    (D) Writing a report.

49. (　　) What does the man offer?
    (A) To write the report.
    (B) To explain psychometrics.
    (C) To chastise Mr. Roberts.
    (D) To read the woman's first draft of the report.

Questions 50 through 52 *refer to the following conversation.*

W : Hey Bob, it's Alice. Who's in charge of purchasing these days? It's Marge, right? Can I speak with her?

M : That's correct. Marge is in charge of purchasing, but she's off this week. I believe her assistant, Greg, is handling it while she's gone. But… he's out to lunch right now. If you need something urgently, as in this moment, go to Pauline in accounting. She can sign off on it.

W : That's OK. No need to go through all that. Do you happen to have Greg's extension?
M : It's 882.

50. (　　) Who does the woman ask to speak with?
    (A) Pauline.
    (B) Greg.
    (C) Marge.
    (D) Bob.

51. (　　) Who is Greg?
    (A) Pauline's assistant.
    (B) Alice's assistant.
    (C) Marge's assistant.
    (D) Bob's assistant.

52. (   ) What does the woman imply?
      (A) She's not in a hurry to solve her problem.
      (B) She's tired of people going on vacation.
      (C) She's afraid of Pauline.
      (D) She's under a lot of pressure.

Questions 53 through 55 *refer to the following conversation between three speakers.*

M : Welcome to The Great American Print Shop. How can I help you?
Woman UK : Hi, I'd like to have some flyers printed for a music festival.

M : No problem. This binder contains our design templates for you to choose from.
Woman UK : Actually, I have a hard copy of the design we'd like to use. It's on this USB flash drive.

M : Oh, a shop policy is that customers use one of our design templates because our software is set up for those templates, but let me ask the manager. Suzanne, this customer has her own design. Is that allowed?
Woman US : It is, but it'll cost a bit more because the design will have to be manually entered.

Woman UK : OK, I don't mind paying extra, but can I get an estimate of how much extra that will cost?

53. (   ) What are the speakers mainly discussing?
      (A) An online payment.
      (B) A store refund.
      (C) A computer upgrade.
      (D) A printing order.

54. (   ) What store policy is mentioned?
      (A) Services must be paid for in cash.
      (B) Deliveries must be scheduled in advance.
      (C) Customers must use a shop design.
      (D) Customers must have a shop account.

55. (   ) What does the manager explain to the customer?
      (A) An extra charge will be added.
      (B) An account has been suspended.
      (C) A warranty cannot be extended.
      (D) Replacement parts have not arrived.

GO ON TO THE NEXT PAGE.

Questions 56 through 58 _refer to the following conversation._

W : Haven't we met? You're Kahlil Amad from Krunk and Wagg, aren't you? I'm Paige Turner, counsel for Smith, Smith and Joans.

M : Oh, right, of course I remember you, Paige. We met at the Bar Association fundraiser in Peoria. You work with Terry Bull, my roommate from law school. How is Terry, by the way?

W : You have a great memory, Kahlil. Terry's doing great, actually. He's up for partner this year.

M : The guy is one of the most talented litigators in the business. You guys are lucky to have him.

56. (   ) Who are the speakers?
     (A) Teachers.
     (B) Volunteers.
     (C) Lawyers.
     (D) Journalists.

57. (   ) How does the man know Terry Bull?
     (A) They were roommates in law school.
     (B) They are from the same town.
     (C) They work for the same company.
     (D) They both dated Paige Turner.

58. (   ) What does the woman say about Terry Bull?
     (A) He's in line for a promotion.
     (B) He's a talented judge.
     (C) He's in Peoria.
     (D) He's got an unfortunate name.

Questions 59 through 61 _refer to the following conversation._

M : Thank you for calling the Apex customer care hotline. How may I help you today?

W : My purse was recently stolen. I need to cancel my Apex Visa card and have a new one sent to me.

M : I'm sorry to hear about that. Give me just one moment. OK, what is the name on the account?

W : Jame Smith. S-M-I-T-H.

59. (   ) What problem does the woman have?
     (A) She lost a close relative.
     (B) Her credit card was stolen.
     (C) The credit card was declined in a restaurant.
     (D) Thieves ransacked her apartment.

60. (　　) What does the woman want to do?
    (A) Get a credit extension.
    (B) Report a suspicious character.
    (C) Buy a new purse.
    (D) Cancel a stolen credit card.

61. (　　) What does the woman imply?
    (A) She misplaced the credit card.
    (B) The credit card was in the stolen purse.
    (C) Her spending limit is too low.
    (D) Everything is always her fault.

Questions 62 through 64 _refer to the following conversation._

M : Thank you for calling Universal Bank. How may I direct your call?

W : Um, yes, like, um, I don't remember my PIN number for my debit card.

M : OK, ma'am. I'll transfer your call to a customer service agent. Do you happen to have the card with you?

W : I think so. Wait. This is Universal Bank? Oh, I thought I was calling United Bank. My mistake.

62. (　　) What is the woman's problem?
    (A) She lost her debit card.
    (B) She forgot her PIN number.
    (C) She is lost.
    (D) She can't access her accounts.

63. (　　) What does the man ask?
    (A) If the woman has an account with Universal Bank.
    (B) If the woman knows her PIN number.
    (C) If the woman can wait while he transfers the call.
    (D) If the woman has the debit card in her possession.

64. (　　) Who does the woman need to speak with?
    (A) A sales representative.
    (B) Someone at United Bank.
    (C) The man's superior.
    (D) A Universal Bank customer service agent.

GO ON TO THE NEXT PAGE.

M : Do you have big plans for the holiday?

W : No, not really. We're going to keep it simple this year. None of the usual festivities.

M : I hear you. Times are tight. My wife and I aren't even exchanging gifts this year.

W : Neither are we. Of course, we are still going to have Christmas for the kids, but otherwise, we're playing it low key.

65. (   ) What are the speakers discussing?
    (A) Gift-giving ideas.
    (B) Holiday plans.
    (C) The state of the economy.
    (D) Their kids.

66. (   ) What does the woman imply?
    (A) Her family will not have an extravagant holiday celebration this year.
    (B) Her holiday plans are complicated.
    (C) Her kids are spoiled and rude.
    (D) Her husband is a cheapskate who doesn't believe in Santa Claus.

67. (   ) What does the man imply?
    (A) He and his wife aren't getting along.
    (B) He is trying to lose weight.
    (C) He doesn't have a lot of money to spend on gifts.
    (D) He never really liked the Christmas season.

Man UK : Hi, Charlotte. I have a question about new hires here at the television station.

W : Sure, Ethan. What's your question?

Man UK : Well, I think a former colleague of mine would be a good fit for our team. She's looking for a new content producer position and we've got an opening in our department. How can I recommend her for the job?

W : Good question. Ah... let's see. Oliver has been here a long time.

Man US : Yes, did I just hear my name?

W : Yes. Do you know how to refer job candidates to the HR department?

Man US : Sure, go to the company website. Find the human resources link, select referrals and download the form. Fill it out and submit it to Carol in HR. She'll take it from there.

68. (　　) What does Ethan want to do?
   (A) Attend a live broadcast.
   (B) Request a transfer.
   (C) Change a work shift.
   (D) Refer a friend for employment.

69. (　　) Why does the woman say, "Oliver has been here a long time."?
   (A) To indicate that Oliver could answer a question.
   (B) To suggest that Oliver be promoted.
   (C) To explain a project Oliver is working on.
   (D) To express surprise about a mistake Oliver made.

70. (　　) What does Oliver recommend doing?
   (A) Consulting an organization chart.
   (B) Speaking to a manager.
   (C) Visiting a website.
   (D) Picking up an employee handbook.

PART 4

***Questions 71 through 73** refer to the following introduction.*

Our next guest is making her third appearance on the program and describes herself as an "ordinary housewife" who did something extraordinary. She is the author of a children's book that became an international bestseller and is now a popular movie. Just four years ago, P.J. Adams was a stay-at-home mother of three when she began writing *The Wizards of Weird*, in her words, "to kill time." Writing the book while waiting to pick up her kids from day care, at night after they were asleep, and in spare moments at basketball games and school plays, Adams never dreamed she'd be writing books professionally. Now she's here to promote the sequel, *The Importance of Being Weird*, due out next month, but she insists that success hasn't changed her. We'll see about that. She's still a devoted mother and wife. Ladies and gentleman, please welcome P.J. Adams.

GO ON TO THE NEXT PAGE.

71. (　　) Who is being introduced?
    (A) An actor.
    (B) An author.
    (C) A politician.
    (D) A movie director.

72. (　　) What will P.J. Adams most likely talk about?
    (A) Her education.
    (B) Her new book.
    (C) Her religion.
    (D) Her children.

73. (　　) How many times has P.J. Adams appeared on the program prior to this introduction?
    (A) Never.
    (B) One.
    (C) Two.
    (D) A dozen.

Questions 74 through 76 are based on the following advertisement.

Are you tired of outrageous winter heating bills? Wouldn't you rather spend that money on something else? Then remember two words: Pella Windows. Pella's double-pane glass traps heat inside your home, so your furnace works less and you save money. We're so confident in our windows that Pella guarantees, in writing, that you will save at least 50 percent on your next heating bill or we'll pay the difference. That's right: 50 percent, or Pella pays. Guaranteed. Not only that, but if you call today, we'll give you 25 percent off our normal installation price when you buy four or more windows. Our professional crews make installation quick and easy. So what are you waiting for? Don't be stuck with huge heating bills this winter. Call Pella Windows today at 777-2354 for a free in-home estimate. That's 777-2354. Pella Windows.

74. (　　) What is being advertised?
    (A) Carpeting.
    (B) Furniture.
    (C) Home appliances.
    (D) Windows.

75. (　　) What does Pella guarantee?
   (A) Complete customer satisfaction.
   (B) Savings of 50 percent on heating bills.
   (C) Shatter-proof glass.
   (D) Same day installation.

76. (　　) How much can the consumer save on installation?
   (A) 20 percent.
   (B) 25 percent.
   (C) 40 percent.
   (D) 50 percent.

Questions 77 through 79 *refer to the following message.*

Hello, Ms. White. This is Joe Lewis from Lewis Construction returning your phone call. You had a couple of questions about the estimate we gave you to remodel your office. First, yes, the quote for the conference room does include installing new carpet and windows. Sorry if that wasn't clear on the estimate. You had also asked why we quoted a range for the cost of lighting. That's because it depends on the type and style of lights you decide you want. The low figure is for standard lighting, and the high one is for the track lighting. As for painting, we subcontract that, so I'll have to check with my painters and see when they can come give you an estimate—hopefully by the end of the week. I'll get back in touch with you about that later today. If you have more questions, give me a call or shoot me an e-mail. My cell phone number is 312-666-0999, and the office is 312-666-0998. E-mail is joe at lewis dot com. Thanks, Ms. White, and have a good day.

77. (　　) What is the main purpose of the message?
   (A) To make a bid.
   (B) To file an estimate.
   (C) To apologize for a mistake.
   (D) To answer questions.

78. (　　) What is not included in the estimate?
   (A) Carpeting in the conference room.
   (B) A range of different types of lighting.
   (C) Painting costs.
   (D) New windows in the conference room.

GO ON TO THE NEXT PAGE.

79. (   ) What does the speaker say Ms. White can do?
    (A) Write a check.
    (B) Call him back.
    (C) Negotiate with the painters.
    (D) Give an estimate.

Questions 80 through 82 *refer to the following recording.*

That's a fair question, and not to be glib but the answer is yes, some of you are going to be out of a job before the end of the year. But we have a plan. Now, in this tough economy, we're going to act just like our customers—tightening our belt and looking for ways to save money. We'll be looking at ways we can conserve energy, operate our stores more efficiently, and integrate new procedures that cut labor costs. We're also going to re-examine our pricing structure. We might have to lower prices and operate on a thinner profit margin for a while. Now, we value each and every one of our employees, and we won't let any one of you go until we've first tried everything we possibly can. So I can't say who among you will be laid off, but rest assured that we're committed to avoiding it at all costs.

80. (   ) Who is the speaker?
    (A) A corporate executive.
    (B) A sales clerk.
    (C) A cashier.
    (D) A parking lot attendant.

81. (   ) What is the speaker talking about?
    (A) Shoplifting.
    (B) Advertising.
    (C) Health care.
    (D) Saving money.

82. (   ) Which of the following is NOT part of the speaker's plan?
    (A) Cutting labor costs.
    (B) Conserving energy.
    (C) Reducing profit margins.
    (D) Hiring new employees.

As you know, we've got a deal with ABC Technology School to provide discount computer classes for our staff. Even though these classes are free to our employees, some of you have complained that workers in your department aren't taking advantage of them. Staff have complained that they are too tired and too busy to drive to the ABC campus after work. But I have a hunch that most of them don't recognize the benefit expanded computer skills will have for their job performance. I can understand this, since most of them already have the skill they need to perform their current jobs well. So, we've decided to be proactive and bring the classes to the employees. Starting immediately, ABC will send an instructor to our offices for twice-weekly classes.

83. (   ) Who is the speaker most likely talking to?
    (A) Department managers.
    (B) New employees.
    (C) Stockholders.
    (D) Computer instructors.

84. (   ) Why are some staff members not taking advantage of the classes?
    (A) They can't afford them.
    (B) They are not convenient.
    (C) They start too early.
    (D) They don't like the instructors.

85. (   ) What did the speaker do to solve the problem?
    (A) He arranged for on-site classes.
    (B) He cancelled the classes.
    (C) He gave bonuses.
    (D) He made attendance mandatory.

Questions 86 through 88 *refer to the following traffic report.*

This is Ursula Ogden with a 3 p.m. KPIX traffic update. At the moment there is a huge backup on southbound Interstate 5 near the MacArthur Avenue exit, due to a car-truck collision. Police and emergency crews are on the scene, and it looks like it's going to take awhile to clear it up. The right two lanes are blocked, but the two left lanes are open, and there's a police officer directing vehicles. Northbound traffic on 5 is also

GO ON TO THE NEXT PAGE.

bottle-necking through that area as drivers slow to take a look. But that congestion should ease in a few minutes, as we see traffic authorities getting ready to switch the special express lanes from southbound to northbound at 3:30. Traffic on other major roadways looks normal at this hour. This is Ursula Ogden and you're listening to KPIX. Traffic is brought to you by Tasty Oatmeal, the breakfast that provides a full day's supply of 14 vitamins and iron. It's not just oatmeal, it's tasty! Stay tuned for news and weather after this word from our sponsor.

86. (   ) When was this report made?
     (A) At dawn.
     (B) Mid-morning.
     (C) Noon.
     (D) Mid-afternoon.

87. (   ) What is causing the back-up in the northbound lanes of Interstate 5?
     (A) People slowing down to look at the accident in the southbound lanes.
     (B) Police and emergency crews.
     (C) Tasty Oatmeal.
     (D) An overturned truck carrying thousands of empty bottles.

88. (   ) What will listeners hear next?
     (A) An advertisement.
     (B) The weather report.
     (C) The traffic report.
     (D) A musical performance.

Questions 89 through 91 *are based on the following announcement.*

Thank you all for coming. After considering several factors, including the survey you completed last quarter, we've decided to implement four-day workweeks, beginning next month. We will operate 10 hours a day, from 8 a.m. to 7 p.m., of course with an hour for lunch, on Monday through Thursday. The office will be closed Fridays and throughout the weekend. Though we will still work 40 hours a week, we estimate that this change will reduce our energy use by 30 percent, and will also save each of you, on average, about $50 a month in gas and transportation costs. Overall, this change will significantly reduce our company's carbon footprint. To save even more energy, we will be installing energy-efficient fluorescent light bulbs throughout the building, starting next week.

During the changeover period, we understand that some of you, particularly those with young children, might need special accommodations as you adjust to a four-day week. We'll be happy to help you any way we can.

89. (　　) What is the speaker announcing?
    (A) A change of working hours.
    (B) A plan to consume more energy.
    (C) A daycare program for employees with young kids.
    (D) A new questionnaire to be passed out.

90. (　　) What will happen on Fridays?
    (A) A government official will visit the campus.
    (B) The light bulbs will be changed.
    (C) The office will be closed.
    (D) Employees will go home at 6:00 p.m.

91. (　　) How many hours will employees now work per week?
    (A) 10.
    (B) 15.
    (C) 20.
    (D) 40.

Questions 92 through 94 refer to the following advertisement.

Are you happy with your current job? Maybe it's time for a change? We can help. I'm Sammy Govic, president of Career Match dot com, and now is a great time to let us help you search for the career you've always dreamed of. Our professional staff will assist you step by step in updating your resume, posting it online, answering ads, and searching through thousands of job listings on your behalf. Instead of wasting your time reading hundreds of advertisements, let us show you how to focus your search on only the most promising leads. We'll keep you updated on the latest employment trends, and teach you how to write an eye-catching resume that will increase your chances of scoring an interview. In fact, we'll even train you in interview techniques. We've placed thousands of people over the past 10 years. What are you waiting for? Call us now at 1-800-929-9292, or visit us online at Career Match dot com.

GO ON TO THE NEXT PAGE.

92. (　　) What is being advertised?
    (A) A product.
    (B) A service.
    (C) A school.
    (D) A job opening.

93. (　　) What is suggested about Career Match dot com?
    (A) It is local.
    (B) It is affordable.
    (C) It is old.
    (D) It is effective.

94. (　　) What does the speaker suggest listeners do?
    (A) Give their two-week notice.
    (B) Send in their resumes.
    (C) Call or visit the website.
    (D) Show up on time.

***Questions 95 through 97** refer to the following tour information and brochure.*

OK, folks. Can I have your attention at the front of the bus? I hope everybody enjoyed our architectural tour of the historic Greenbriar District. We saw some amazing stuff, didn't we? Now if you look to the right, you'll see the Shipley's Inn, where we'll have lunch. Constructed in 1835, it was originally the county courthouse. And according to our schedule, we're right on time. As you get off the bus, I'll pass out brochures with information about what you'll be seeing in the Sears Building, home of the city's largest newspaper. Also, let me remind you; do not leave any personal items on the bus when we disembark, and keep track of those personal belongings throughout the tour.

95. (　　) What does the speaker say about Shipley's Inn?
    (A) It serves exotic food.
    (B) It has multiple locations in the area.
    (C) It used to be a courthouse.
    (D) It has recently won an award.

96. (   ) Look at the graphic. What time is this talk most likely being given?
  (A) At 10:00 A.M.
  (B) At 12:00 P.M.
  (C) At 1:15 P.M.
  (D) At 4:00 P.M.

```
┌─────────────────────────────────────────────┐
│                                             │
│   TOUR SCHEDULE                             │
│   --------------------------------          │
│   Greenbriar District  10:00 A.M.           │
│   Lunch  12:00 P.M.                         │
│   Sears Building  1:15 P.M.                 │
│   Exploration Museum  4:00 P.M.             │
│                                             │
│   =============================             │
└─────────────────────────────────────────────┘
```

97. (   ) What does the speaker say she will distribute?
  (A) Bottles of water.
  (B) Maps.
  (C) Brochures.
  (D) Umbrellas.

Questions 98 through 100 *refer to the following excerpt from a meeting and garden layout.*

Thanks for attending this planning meeting for the new community garden. I'm Edward, and I'm the coordinator of this project. Here's the layout for the new garden. We'll mostly be planting perennial flowers and ornamental shrubs, but we will have a vegetable garden, too, and we're going to plant that first. The vegetables are going to go in the plot immediately to the left as you enter the garden. Also, I need volunteers to help me on Saturday. I'd like to put up a fence around the perimeter of the garden. The wood for the fence will be delivered that morning.

98. (   ) Who is the speaker?
  (A) A security guard.
  (B) A project coordinator.
  (C) A course instructor.
  (D) A news journalist.

GO ON TO THE NEXT PAGE.

99. (   ) Look at the graphic. Where will vegetables be planted?
  (A) Plot 1.
  (B) Plot 2.
  (C) Plot 3.
  (D) Plot 4.

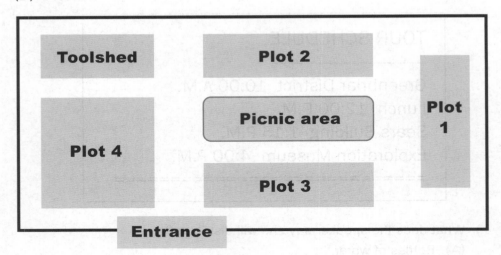

100. (   ) What does the speaker plan to do on Saturday?
  (A) Take some photographs.
  (B) Install a fence.
  (C) Lead a tour.
  (D) Attend a picnic.

TOEIC ANSWER SHEET

REGISTRATION No.

姓 名
N A M E

LISTENING SECTION

Part 1

No.	ANSWER
1	A B C D
2	A B C D
3	A B C D
4	A B C D
5	A B C D
6	A B C D
7	A B C D
8	A B C D
9	A B C D
10	A B C D

Part 2

No.	ANSWER	No.	ANSWER
11	A B C D	21	A B C D
12	A B C D	22	A B C D
13	A B C D	23	A B C D
14	A B C D	24	A B C D
15	A B C D	25	A B C D
16	A B C D	26	A B C D
17	A B C D	27	A B C D
18	A B C D	28	A B C D
19	A B C D	29	A B C D
20	A B C D	30	A B C D

Part 3

No.	ANSWER	No.	ANSWER	No.	ANSWER
31	A B C D	41	A B C D	51	A B C D
32	A B C D	42	A B C D	52	A B C D
33	A B C D	43	A B C D	53	A B C D
34	A B C D	44	A B C D	54	A B C D
35	A B C D	45	A B C D	55	A B C D
36	A B C D	46	A B C D	56	A B C D
37	A B C D	47	A B C D	57	A B C D
38	A B C D	48	A B C D	58	A B C D
39	A B C D	49	A B C D	59	A B C D
40	A B C D	50	A B C D	60	A B C D

Part 4

No.	ANSWER	No.	ANSWER	No.	ANSWER	No.	ANSWER
61	A B C D	71	A B C D	81	A B C D	91	A B C D
62	A B C D	72	A B C D	82	A B C D	92	A B C D
63	A B C D	73	A B C D	83	A B C D	93	A B C D
64	A B C D	74	A B C D	84	A B C D	94	A B C D
65	A B C D	75	A B C D	85	A B C D	95	A B C D
66	A B C D	76	A B C D	86	A B C D	96	A B C D
67	A B C D	77	A B C D	87	A B C D	97	A B C D
68	A B C D	78	A B C D	88	A B C D	98	A B C D
69	A B C D	79	A B C D	89	A B C D	99	A B C D
70	A B C D	80	A B C D	90	A B C D	100	A B C D

READING SECTION

Part 5

No.	ANSWER
101	A B C D
102	A B C D
103	A B C D
104	A B C D
105	A B C D
106	A B C D
107	A B C D
108	A B C D
109	A B C D
110	A B C D

Part 6

No.	ANSWER	No.	ANSWER
111	A B C D	121	A B C D
112	A B C D	122	A B C D
113	A B C D	123	A B C D
114	A B C D	124	A B C D
115	A B C D	125	A B C D
116	A B C D	126	A B C D
117	A B C D	127	A B C D
118	A B C D	128	A B C D
119	A B C D	129	A B C D
120	A B C D	130	A B C D

Part 7

No.	ANSWER	No.	ANSWER	No.	ANSWER
131	A B C D	141	A B C D	151	A B C D
132	A B C D	142	A B C D	152	A B C D
133	A B C D	143	A B C D	153	A B C D
134	A B C D	144	A B C D	154	A B C D
135	A B C D	145	A B C D	155	A B C D
136	A B C D	146	A B C D	156	A B C D
137	A B C D	147	A B C D	157	A B C D
138	A B C D	148	A B C D	158	A B C D
139	A B C D	149	A B C D	159	A B C D
140	A B C D	150	A B C D	160	A B C D

No.	ANSWER	No.	ANSWER	No.	ANSWER	No.	ANSWER
161	A B C D	171	A B C D	181	A B C D	191	A B C D
162	A B C D	172	A B C D	182	A B C D	192	A B C D
163	A B C D	173	A B C D	183	A B C D	193	A B C D
164	A B C D	174	A B C D	184	A B C D	194	A B C D
165	A B C D	175	A B C D	185	A B C D	195	A B C D
166	A B C D	176	A B C D	186	A B C D	196	A B C D
167	A B C D	177	A B C D	187	A B C D	197	A B C D
168	A B C D	178	A B C D	188	A B C D	198	A B C D
169	A B C D	179	A B C D	189	A B C D	199	A B C D
170	A B C D	180	A B C D	190	A B C D	200	A B C D

「多益獎學金」申請辦法：

★凡向學習出版公司團訂New TOEIC Model Test課堂教材的同學，參加TOEIC測驗，成績達下列標準，可申請以下獎學金。

分 數	獎 學 金
990分滿分	2萬元現金支票
950分以上	1萬元現金支票
900分以上	5,000元現金支票
800分以上	1,000元現金支票
700分以上	500元現金支票

1. 同一級分獎學金，不得重複申請；申請第二次獎學金時，則須先扣除已領取的部份，補足差額。
   例如：某生第一次參加多益測驗，得分825，可申請獎學金1,000元，之後第二次參加測驗，得分950，則某生可領取
   10,000元 – 1,000元 = 9,000元獎學金差額。

2. 若同學申請第一次獎學金後，考第二次成績比第一次差，雖仍達到申請獎學金標準，將不得再申請獎學金。

3. 申請同學須於上課期間，憑成績單申請，並有授課老師簽名。

【本活動於2021年12月31日截止】